About the Illustrator

Name:

Age: _____ Hometown:

Something I love doing with my mom is:

My mom's biggest talent is:

The best vacation we ever took together was:

Amazing Mom

COMPENDIUM®

kids

inspiring possibilities.™

This is my mom. She's amazing.

When the weather is stormy, she can make the rain stop and the sun come out.

She might even make a rainbow if she isn't too busy that day.

And she bakes such delicious desserts that I'll do *anything* to have one more bite.

When my mom plants seeds,
they grow really big.

Her flowers don't look like anything anyone has ever seen before.

When my mom tells me bedtime stories,

the characters come to life
right there in my room!

Sometimes, after the story is finished, she even lets them sleep over.

My mom can make even the most grumpy monster smile.

And her hugs
have magical powers.

She can heal any hurt faster than anything I know.

My mom has the most important job in the world.

WITH SPECIAL THANKS TO THE
ENTIRE COMPENDIUM FAMILY.

CREDITS:

Written by: M.H. Clark
Designed by: Julie Flahiff
Edited by: Amelia Riedler

ISBN: 978-1-938298-21-9

1st printing. Printed in China with soy inks. A011310001